I0615293

Herbert G. Wells

Select Conversations with an Uncle

Herbert G. Wells

Select Conversations with an Uncle

ISBN/EAN: 9783337275334

Printed in Europe, USA, Canada, Australia, Japan

Cover: Foto ©Andreas Hilbeck / pixelio.de

More available books at **www.hansebooks.com**

THE MAYFAIR SET

III
CONVERSATIONS
WITH AN
UNCLE

SELECT
CONVERSATIONS
WITH
AN UNCLE
(NOW EXTINCT)

and two other
reminiscences by

·H·G·WELLS·

LONDON:
JOHN LANE·

NEW YORK ···
THE MERRIAM
COMPANY

1895···

Second Edition

TO

MY DEAREST

AND BEST FRIEND,

R. A. C

PREFATORY

HE was, I remember, short, but by no means conspicuously short, and of a bright, almost juvenile, complexion, very active in his movements and garrulous—or at least very talkative. His judgments were copious and frequent in the old days, and some at least I found entertaining. At times his fluency was really remarkable. He had a low opinion of eminent people—a thing I have been careful to suppress, and his dissertations had ever an irresponsible gaiety of manner that may have blinded me to their true want of merit. That, I say, was in the old days, before his abrupt extinction, before the cares of this world suddenly sprang upon, and choked him. I would listen to him cheerfully, and afterwards I would go away and make articles out of him for the

Pall Mall Gazette, so adding a certain material advantage to my mental and moral benefit. But all that has gone now, to my infinite regret; and sorrowing, I have arranged this unworthy little tribute to his memory, this poor dozen of casual monologues that were so preserved. The merits of the monument are his entirely; its faults entirely my own.

CONTENTS

CONTENTS

OF CONVERSATION AND THE ANATOMY OF FASHION

THIS uncle of mine, you must understand, having attained—by the purest accident —some trifles of distinction and a certain affluence in South Africa, came over at the earliest opportunity to London to be photographed and lionised. He took to fame easily, as one who had long prepared in secret. He lurked in my chambers for a week while the new dress suit was a-making—his old one I really had to remonstrate against—and then we went out to be admired. During the week's retirement he secreted quite a wealth of things to say—appropriate remarks on edibles, on music, on popular books, on conversation, off-hand little things, jotting them down in a note-book as they came into his mind, for he had a high conception of social intercourse, and the public expectation. He was ever a methodical little gentleman, and all these accumulations that he could not get into his talk, he proposed to put away for the big volume of " Reminiscences " that was to round off his life. At last he was a mere conversational firework, crammed with latent wit and jollity, and ready to blaze and sparkle in fizzing style as soon as the light of social intercourse should touch him.

But after we had circulated for a week or so, my uncle began to manifest symptoms of distress. He had not had a chance. People did not seem to talk at all in his style. "Where do the literary people meet together, George ? I am afraid you have chosen your friends ill. Surely those long-haired serious people who sat round my joke like old cats round a beetle—what is it ?—were not the modern representatives of a *salon*. Those abominable wig-makers' eccentricities who talked journalistic 'shop,' and posed all over that preposterous room with the draperies! Those hectic young men who have done nothing except run down everybody! Don't tell me that is the literary society of London, George. Where do they let off wit now, George? Where do they sparkle? I want to sparkle. Badly. I shall burst, George, if I don't."

Now really, you know, there are no *salons* now—I suppose we turn all our conversation into "copy"—or the higher education has eliminated the witty woman —and my uncle became more and more distressed. He said a lot of his good things to me, which was sheer waste. I became afraid. I got him all the introductions I could, pushed him into every lion's den I had access to. But there was no relief.

"I see what it is, George," said my uncle, "these literary people write themselves out. They say nothing for private use. Their brains are weary when they come into company. They get up in the morning fresh and bright, and write, write, write. Then, when they are jaded, they condescend to social intercourse. It is their way of resting. But why don't they go to bed? No more clever people for me, George. Let us try the smart. Perhaps among them we shall find smart talking still surviving. *Allons*, George!"

That is how my uncle came into collision with fashion, how I came to take him to the Fitz-Brilliants.

Of course you have heard of the Fitz-Brilliants? If you have not, it is not their fault. They are the smartest people in London. Always hard at work, keeping up to date, are the Fitz-Brilliants. But my uncle did not appreciate them. Worse! They did not appreciate my uncle. He came to me again, more pent up than ever, and the thing I had feared happened. He began to discourse to me. It was about Fashion, with a decided reference to the Fitz-Brilliants, and some reflections upon the alleys of literary ability and genius I had taken him through.

"George," said my uncle, "*this Fashion*

is just brand-new vulgarity. It is merely the regal side of the medal. The Highly Fashionable and the Absolutely Vulgar are but two faces of the common coin of humanity, struck millions at a time. Spin the thing in the light of wealth, and I defy you, as it whizzes from the illumination of riches to the shadow of poverty, to distinguish the one stamp from the other. You cannot say, here the *mode* ends, and there the unspeakable thing, its counterpart, has its beginning. Their distinction of mere position has vanished, and they are in seeming as in substance one and indivisible."

My uncle was now fairly under way.

" The fashionable is the foam on the ocean of vulgarity, George, cast up by the waves of that ocean, and caught by the light of the sun. It is the vulgar— blossoming. The flower it is of that earthly plant, destined hereafter to run to seed, and to beget new groves and thickets, new jungles, of vulgar things.

" Note, George, how true this is of

that common property of the vulgar and
fashionable—slang. The apt phrase falls
and applause follows, and then down it
goes. The essential feature of slang is
words misapplied ; the essential distinction of a coarse mind from one refined,
an inability to appreciate fine distinctions
and minor discords ; the essential of the
vulgar, good example misused. First the ᷍
fashionable get the apt phrase, and bandy
it about in inapt connections until even
the novelty of its discordance has ceased
to charm, and thereafter it sinks down,
down. *Fin de siècle* and *cliché* have,
for instance, passed downward from the
courts of the fashionable among journalists
into the unspeakable depths below. Soon,
if not already, *fin de siècle* gin and
onions and haddocks will be for sale in
the Whitechapel-road, and Harriet will
be calling Billy a " cliché faced swine."
Even so do ostrich feathers begin a career
of glory at the Drawing-Room and the
fashionable photographer's, and, after end-
less re-dyeing, come to their last pose

before a Hampstead camera on a bright
Bank Holiday.

" The fashionable and vulgar are after
all but the expression of man's gregarious
instinct.　Every poor mortal is torn by
the conflicting dreads of being ' commonplace,' and of being ' eccentric.'　He, and
more particularly she, is continually imitat-
ing and avoiding imitation, trying to be
singular and yet like other people.　In
the exquisitely fashionable and in the
entirely vulgar the sheep-like longing is
triumphant, and the revolting individual
has disappeared.　The former is a
mechanical vehicle upon which the new
' correct thing' rides forth, to extort the
astonishment of men ; the latter a life-
less bier bearing its corrupt and unre-
cognisable remains away to final oblivion,
amidst universal execration.

"It is curious to notice, George, that there
has of late been a fashion in ' originality.'
The commonplace has turned, as it were,
upon itself, and vehemently denied its
identity.　So that people who were not

eccentric have become rare, and genius, so far as it is a style of hairdressing, and originality, so far as it is a matter of etiquette or morals, have become the habitual garments of the commonplace. The introduction of the word 'bourgeois' as a comminatory epithet into the English language, by bourgeois writers writing for the bourgeois, will remain a memorial for ever, for the philological humourist to chuckle over. If good resolutions could change the natures of men, opinion has lately set so decidedly against the fashionable and the vulgar that their continued existence in this world would be very doubtful. But the leopard cannot change his spots so easily. While the stars go on in their courses, until the cooling of the earth puts an end to the career of life, and the last trace of his ancestral tendency to imitation disappears as the last man becomes an angel, depend upon it, George, the fashionable will ever pursue this chimæra of distinguished correctness, and trail the inseparable howling vulgar in its wake—for ever chased, like a dog with a tin can attached, by the horror of its own tail."

Thus my uncle. He had said a few of his things. It is possible his trick of talking like a disarticulated essay had something to do with his social discomfort. But anyhow he seemed all the better for the release.

"Talking of tails, George," he said, "reminds me. I noticed the men at the Fitz-Brilliants' had their coats cut—well, I should say, just a half inch shorter here than this of mine. Your man is not up to date. I must get the thing altered to-morrow."

THE THEORY OF THE PERPETUAL DISCOMFORT OF HUMANITY

HE had been sitting with his feet upon the left jamb of my mantel, admiring the tips of his shoes in silence for some time.

"George," he said, dropping his cigar-ash thoughtfully into my inkstand, in order, I imagine, to save my carpet, "have you ever done pioneer work for Humanity?"

"Never," I said. "How do you get that sort of work?"

"I don't know. I met a man and a woman, though, the other night, who said they were engaged in that kind of thing. It seems to me to be exhausting work, and it makes the hair very untidy. They do it chiefly with their heads. It consists, so I understand, of writing stuff in a hurry, rushing about in cabs, wearing your hair in some unpleasant manner, and holding disorderly meetings."

" Who are these people ? "

" Never heard of them before, though they told me they were quite well known. The lady asked me if I had been to Chicago."

I chuckled. I could imagine no more hideous insult to my uncle.

" I told her that I had been to most places south-eastward and eastward, but never across the Atlantic. She informed me that I ought to have gone to Chicago, and that America was a great country, and I remarked that I had always thought it was so great that one could best appreciate it at a distance. Then she asked me what I thought of the condition of the lower classes, and I told her I was persuaded, from various things I had noticed, that a lot of them were frightfully hard up. And with that she started off to show whose fault it was, by the Socratic method."

" Entertaining ? "

" A little. I did not get all my answers

right.   For instance, when she asked, 'Who sends the members of Parliament to Westminster?' I answered her, 'The governors of the young ones and the wives of the others.'   And when she said that was wrong—I don't remember Socrates ever saying bluntly that an answer was wrong—I said I supposed she referred to the Evil One.   It was very dull of me, of course, and it obliged her to dictate the right solution.

"Afterwards she threw over teaching me anything, and explained to me all about her Movements.   At least, I got really interested in her Movements.   One thing she said struck me very much, though it could hardly be called novel.   It was that the fads of one age were the fashions of the next; that while the majority of people were engaged in their little present-day chores, persons like herself are making the laws and preparing the customs for the generation to follow."

"Poor generations to follow!" I said.

"Yes, but there is a lot of truth in it;

and do you know there flashed upon me
all at once a great theory, the Theory of
the Perpetual Discomfort of Humanity.
Just let me explain it to you, George,"
he said, bringing himself round so that
his legs hung over the arm of his chair.
" I think you will see I have made a
very great discovery, gone to the root of
the whole of this bother of reform move-
ment, advancement of humanity, and the
rest of it." He sucked his cigar for a
moment. "Each age," he said, "has its
own ideals of what constitutes human
happiness."

" A very profound observation," said I.

" Looking down the vista of history,
one may generalise and say that we see
human beings continually troubled by the
conditions under which they live. I can
think of no time in the world when there
was not some Question or other getting
fussed about: at one time episcopal
celibacy, at another time the Pict and
Scot problem, and so on. Always a
crumpled rose-leaf. Hence reform move-

ments. Now, reforms move slowly, and by the time these reforms come about, the people whom they would have made happy, and who fussed and encountered dislike and satire and snubbing, and burning and boiling in oil, and suchlike discouragements, for the sake of them, were dead and buried and mere sanitary problems. The new people had new and quite different needs, and the reforms for which their fathers fought and died more or less uncomfortably, and got into debt with the printers, so soon as there were printers to get into debt with, were about as welcome as belated dinner guests. You take me? Ireland, when Home Rule comes home to it, will simply howl with indignation. And we are living in the embodied discontent of the eighteenth century. Adam Smith, Tom Paine, and Priestley would have looked upon this age and seen that it was good—devilish good; and as you know, George, to us it is— well, a bit of a nuisance anyhow. However, most people are like myself, and try to be as comfortable as they can, and no doubt the next generation might do very well with it. And then the pioneer people begin legislating, agitating, and ordering things differently. As you know, George, I am inclined to conservatism. Constitutionally, I tend to adapt myself to my circumstances. It seems to me so much easier to fit the man to the age than to fit the age to the man. Let us, I say, settle down. We shall never be able to settle down while they keep altering things. It may not be a perfect world, but then I am not a perfect man: Some of the imperfections are, at least, very convenient. So my theory is this: the people whom the age suits fairly well don't bother—*I* don't bother; the others do. It is these confounded glaring and unshorn anachronisms that upset everything. They go about flapping their ideals at you, and writing novels with a motive, and starting movements and societies, and generally poking one's epoch to rags, until at last it is worn out and you have to start a new one. My conception of the progress of humanity is something after the Wandering Jew pattern. Your average humanity I figure as a comfortable person like myself, always trying to sit down and put its legs somewhere out of the way, and being continually stirred up by women in felt hats and short skirts, and haggard men with those beastly, long, insufficient beards, and soulful eyes, and trumpet-headed creatures, and bogles with spectacles and bald heads, and nephews who look at watches. What are you looking at your watch for, George ? I'm very happy as I am.

"Has it ever occurred to you, George, that one of the most uncomfortable things in the world must be to outlive your age ? To have all the reforms of your boyish liberalism coming home to roost, just as you are settling down to the old order. . . .

"Six o'clock, by Jove ! We shall keep them waiting if we don't mind."

"IDEALS!" said my uncle; "certainly Ideals. Of course one must have ideals, else life would be bare materialism. Bare fact alone, naked necessity, is impossible barren rock for a soul to root upon. Life, indeed, is an unfurnished house, an empty glass in a thirsty land—good and necessary for foundation, but insufficient for any satisfaction unless we have ideals. Or, again, ideals are the flesh upon the skeleton of reality, and it cannot live without them.

"It always appears to me," said my uncle, "that the comparison of ideals to furniture is particularly appropriate. They are the draperies of the mind, and they hide the nakedness of truth. Your fireplace is ugly, your mere necessary shelves and seats but planks and crudity, all your surroundings so much office furniture, until the skilful hand and the draperies come in. Then a few cunning loopings and foldings, and behold softness and delicacy, crudity gone, and life well worth the living. So that you cannot value ideals too highly.

" Yet at the same time —— " My uncle became meditative.

" I would not have a man the *slave* of his ideals. Hangings make the room comfortable, but, after all, hangings *are* hangings. Perhaps, now and then — of course, I would not suggest continual inconstancy—a slight change, a little re-arrangement, even a partial replacement, might brighten up the dear old dwelling-place. An ideal may be clung to too fondly. When the moth gets into it, or the dust—did not Carlyle warn us against this, lest they ' accumulate and at last produce suffocation ' ? I am exactly at one with him there.

" And that, as any Cabinet Minister explains every time he opens a public library, is why we have literature. Good

books are the warehouses of ideals. Does
it strike you your furniture is sombre,
a bit Calvinistic and severe—try a statuette
by Pope, or a classical piece out of Heine.
Too much white and gold for every-day
purposes—then the Reverend Laurence
Sterne will oblige. Urban tone may be
corrected by Hardy, and Lowell will give
you urbanity. And, however well you
match and balance them, remember there
is a time for ideals, and a time when
they are better out of the way.

"The Philistine of Victorian literature,
is a person without ideals, the practical
man. But just now the fashion is all for
the things. Ruskin and Carlyle set it
going, and to-day the demand for ideals
exceeds the supply. And as a result,
we meet with innumerable people anxious
to have the correct thing, but a little
unsympathetic or inexpert, and those
unavoidable people who do not like the
things but feel compelled to get them.
Ideals are not the easiest possessions to
have and manage, and they may even rise

to the level of serious inconveniences.   So
that I sometimes wonder these Extension
people have not taken up the subject of
their management and use.

"Note, for instance, the folly of bringing ideals too much into the daily life ;
it is childish, like a baby insisting on its
new toy at meal times, and taking it to
bed.   Never use an ideal as a standard,
and avoid any that reflect upon your con-
duct.   The extremest decorative people
refrain from enamelling their kettles, and
my cook though a 'born lady' does not
wear her silk dress in the kitchen.
Ideals are the full dress of the soul.   A
business man, for instance, who let visions
of reverend Venetian and Genoese seigniors
interfere with his agile City movements—
who, to carry out our comparison, draped
his mind with these things—would be
uncommonly like a bowler in a dressing-
gown.

"Then an ideal, we are also told, is an
elevating influence in life ; but unless one
is very careful one may get hoist with one's

own petard to a pitifully transitory soar above common humanity. The soar itself is not unpleasant, but the sequel is sometimes disagreeable.

" To show how an ideal may trip up an inexpert mortal, take that man Javvers and his wife. She also had an ideal husband, which was, indeed, a kind of bigamy, and her constant references to this creation of hers used to drive poor old Javvers frantic. It became as objectionable as if she had been its sorrowing widow, and ultimately it wrecked the happiness of their little home very completely.

" The seat of ideals, then, in one's mind, should be, as it were, a lounge, over which these hangings may drape and flap harmlessly ; but it may easily become as the bed of Procrustes. To turn ideals to idols, and to command your whole world to bow down to them, savours of the folly of Nebuchadnezzar the king. Let your ideal world be far away from reality, fit it with rococo furniture, angels and birds-of-paradise, Minnesinger flowers and views of the

Delectable Mountains : and go there occa-
sionally and rest—to return without illu-
sions, without encumbrance, but with re-
newed zest, to the sordid world of the
actual, the world of every day.   Herein
is the real use of the ideal; all other is
fanaticism and folly."

THE
ART OF BEING PHOTOGRAPHED

" AN album," said my uncle, as he sat
and turned over my collection of physiog-
nomy, " is, I think, the best reading in the
world.   You get such sidelights on the
owner's heredity, George ; distant cousins
caricature his features and point the moral
of his nose, and ancestral faces prophesy his
fate. His friends, moreover, figure the secret
of his soul. But what a lot we have to learn
yet in the art of being photographed, what
grotesque and awkward blunders your
common sitters make !   Why, for instance,
do men brush their hair so excessively when
they go before the lens ?   Your cousin here
looks like a cheap chess pawn about the head,
whereas as I know him his head is a thing
like a worn-out paint-brush.   Where but
in a photograph would you see a parting

so straight as this ?   It is unnatural.   You
flatten down all a man's character ; for
nothing shows that more than the feathers
and drakes' tails, the artful artlessness, or
revolutionary tumult of his hair.   Mind
you, I am not one of those who would
prohibit a man wearing what he conceives
to be his best clothes to the photographer's.
I like to see the little vanity peeping out—
the last moment's folly of a foolish tie,
nailed up for a lifetime.   Yet all the same,
people should understand that the camera
takes no note of newness, but much of
the cut and fit.   And a man should certainly not go and alter his outline into
a feminine softness, by pouring oil on his
troubled mane and plastering it down with
a brush and comb.   It is not tidiness, but
hypocrisy.

"We have indeed very much to learn in
this matter.   It is a thing that needs teaching, like deportment or dancing.   Plenty of
men I have noticed, who would never do
it in real life, commit the sin of being over-
gentlemanly in an album.   Their clothes

are even indecently immaculate. They become, not portraits, but fashion-plates. I hate a man who is not rumpled and creased a little, as much as I do a brand new pipe. And, as a sad example of sin on the other hand, on the side of carelessness, I have seen renderings of a very august personage indeed, in a hat—a *hat*! It was tilted, and to add to the atrocity, he was holding a cigar. This I regard as horrible. Think! your photograph may go into boudoirs. Imagine Gladys opening the album to Ænone; ' Now I will show you *him.*' And there you sit, leering at their radiant sweetness, hat on, and a cigar reeking between your fingers.

" No, George, a man should go very softly to a photographer's, and he should sit before the camera with reverence in his heart and in his attitude, as if he were in the presence of the woman he loved."

He turned to Mrs Harborough's portrait, looked at it, hesitated, looked again, and passed on.

" I often think we do not take this

business of photography in a sufficiently
serious spirit. Issuing a photograph is like
marriage : you can only undo the mischief
with infinite woe. I know of one man
who has an error of youth of this kind on
his mind—a fancy-dress costume affair,
Crusader or Templar—of which he is more
ashamed than many men would be of the
meanest sins. For sometimes the camera
has its mordant moods, and amazes you by
its saturnine estimate of your merits..
This man was perhaps a little out of harmony with the garments of chivalry, and
a trifle complacent and vain at the time.
But the photograph of him is so cynical
and contemptuous, so merciless in its ex-
posure of his element of foolishness, that
we may almost fancy the spook of Carlyle
had got mixed up with the chemicals upon
the film. Yet it never really dawned upon
him until he had distributed this advertise-
ment of his little weakness far and wide, that
the camera had called him a fool to his face.
I believe he would be glad now to buy
them all back at five pounds a copy.

"This of Minnie Hobson is a work of art. Bless me, the girl must be thirty-seven or thirty-eight now, and just look at her ! These photographers have got a trick now, if your face is one of the long kind, of raising the camera, bending your head forward, and firing down at you. So our Minnie becomes quite chubby again. Then, this thing has been retouched." My uncle peered into the photograph. "It seems to me it is pretty nearly all retouching. For instance, if you look at the eye, that high light is not perfectly even ; that was touched in on the negative with a pencil. Then about the neck of our Minnie I have observed certain bones, just the slightest indication of her collar-bone, George, but that has disappeared under the retoucher's pencil. Then the infantile smoothness of her cheek, and the beautifully-rounded outline, is produced by the retoucher carefully scraping off the surface of the film where the cheekbone projected with a sharp knife. There are also in real life little lines between the corner of

our Minnie's mouth and her nostril.   And
again, Minnie is one of those people whose
dresses never seem to fit, but this fits like
a glove.   These retouchers are like Midas,
and they turn all that comes to their hands
to gold ; or, like Spring, the flowers come
back at their approach.   They reverse the
work of Ithuriel, and restore brightness to
the fallen.   They sit at their little desks,
and scratch, scratch, scratch with those
delicate pencils of theirs, scratching away
age, scratching away care, making the
crooked straight, and the rough smooth.
They are the fairies of photography, and
fill our albums with winsome changelings.
Their ministry anticipates in a little way
the angels who will take us when we die,
releasing us from the worn and haggard
body of this death, and showing something of the eternal life and youth that
glows within.   Or one might say that the
spirit of the retoucher is the spirit of Love.
It makes plain women beautiful, and
common men heroic.   Her regal fingers
touch for the evil of ungainliness, and,

behold, we are restored. Her pencil is like the Queen's sword, and it makes knights out of common men.

"When I have my photograph taken," said my uncle, "I always like to think of the retoucher. I idealise her; I fancy her with the sweetest eyes I have ever seen, and an expression infinitely soft and tender. And she looks closely into my face, and her little pencil goes gently and lovingly over my features. Tickle, tickle. In that way, George, I get a really very nice expression indeed." My uncle turned to his own presentment, and mused pleasantly for a space. Then he looked again at Mrs Harborough as if inadvertently, and asked her name.

"I like this newer way of taking your photograph, against a mere grey background; just the head of you. One should always beware of the property furniture of the photographer. In the seventies they were great at such aids—a pedestal, a cork rustic stile, wide landscape in the distance, but I think that we are at

least getting beyond that now.   People in
those days must have been afraid to be
left alone before a camera, or they wanted
it to seem that they were taken unawares,
quite against their modesty—did not know
what the camera was, and were just looking
at it.   A very favourite pose for girls was
a graceful droop over a sofa, chin on
elegant hand.   When I was at Dribble-
bridge—I was a bright young fellow then
—I collected a number of local photographs, ladies chiefly, and the thing was
very noticeable when I put them in a row
over my mantleshelf.   The local 'artist'
was intensely fond of that pose.   But
fancy the local leader finding her cook
drooping over the same sofa as herself !
Nowadays, I see, you get merely the heads
of your girls, with their hair flossed up,
intense light from above, and faces in
shadow.   I think it is infinitely better.

What horrible things hands become in
a photograph !   I wonder how it is that
the hand in a photograph is always four
shades darker than the arm.   Every girl

who goes to be photographed in evening dress should be solemnly warned to keep her hands out of the picture. They will look as though she has been enamelling the grate, or toying with a bucket of pitch. There is something that sins against my conception of womanly purity in those dark hands."

My uncle shut the album. " Yes, it is a neglected field of education, an important branch of deportment altogether forgotten. Our well-bred ease fails us before the camera ; we are lucky if we merely look stiff and self-conscious. I should fancy there would be an opening for some clever woman to teach people how to dress for the occasion and how to sit, what to avoid and how to avoid it. As it is, we go in a state of nervous agitation, obsequiously costumed ; our last vestige of self-assertion vanishes before the unwinking Cyclops eye of the instrument, and we cower at the mercy of the thing and its attendant. They make what they will of us, and the retoucher simply edits the review with an eye to the market. So history is falsified before our faces, and we prepare a lie for our grandchildren. We fail to stamp our individualities upon our photographs, and are mere 'dumb-driven cattle' in the matter. We sin against ourselves in this neglect, and act against the spirit of the age. Sooner or later this haphazard treatment of posterity must come to an end." He meditated for a moment. Then, as if pursuing a train of thought, "That Mrs Harborough is a very pretty woman, George. Where did you happen to meet her?"

BAGSHOT'S MURAL DECORATIONS

BAGSHOT was rather proud of his new quarters until my uncle called upon him. Up to then he felt assured he was doing right ; had, indeed, not the faintest doubt in the matter until my uncle unsettled him. "Nice carpet, Bagshot," said my uncle, "nice and soft. This chair certainly very comfortable. But what the mischief do you mean—you, with your pretence to culture—by hanging your dwelling with all those framed and glazed photograph and autograph dittoes ? I should have thought you at least would have known better. Love and Life, and Love and Death, the Daphnephoria, Rembrandt's portrait—Wild Havoc, man ! What were you thinking of?"

Bagshot seemed staggered. He ventured to intimate feebly his persuasion that the things were rather good.

"Good they certainly are, and well reproduced, but only the Bible and Shakspeare could stand this incessant re-iteration, and not all Shakspeare. These things are in shop windows, man—drawing-rooms, offices, everywhere. They afflict me like popular songs—like popular quotations. They are good enough—as a matter of fact they are too good. Only, don't you know Willis has Love and Life and Love and Death ? And so has Smith, and Bays has Rembrandt's portrait in his office, and my niece Euphemia has the Daphnephoria in her drawing-room. I can't understand, George, why you let it stay there. It is possible to have too much of a good thing. There is no getting away from these all too popular triumphs. They cover up the walls everywhere. They consume all other art. I shall write a schedule some day of the Fifty Correct Pictures of the British People. And to find *you*, Bagshot, among the Philistines !"

"I thought they showed rather an

improvement in the general taste," said Bagshot. "There is no reason why a thing should not be common, and yet very beautiful. Primroses, for instance——"

" That is true enough, but pictures are not primroses," said my uncle. " Besides, I think we like primroses all the better because they must soon be over; but these are perennial blossoms, like the everlasting flowers and dried grass of a lodging house. They may still be beautiful, but by this time, Bagshot, they are awfully dry and dusty. Who looks at them ? I notice our eyes avoid them even while we talk about them. We have all noticed everything there is to be noticed, and said all the possible things that are to be said about them long ago. Surely a picture must be a little fresh to please. Else we shall come at last to the perfect picture, and art will have an end. Don't you see the mere popularity of these things of the pavement is enough to condemn them in the estimation of every right-minded person ? "

" I don't see it," said Bagshot, making head against the torrent. " I cannot afford to go to these swells and get original work of theirs——"

" What do you want with ' these swells' and their original work ? " interrupted my uncle fiercely. " Haven't they used up all their originality ages ago ? Is · it not open to such men as yourself to discover new men ? There are men pining in garrets now for you, Bagshot. Fancy the delight of having pictures that are unfamiliar, pictures that catch the eye and are actually to be looked at, pictures that suggest new remarks, pictures by a name that the stray visitor has never heard of and which therefore puzzle him dreadfully because he hasn't the faintest idea whether to praise or blame them ! Isn't it worth hunting studios for, and even, maybe, going to the Academy ? Besides, suppose your struggling artist comes to the front. What price the five-guinea specimen of his early style then ? Your artistic virtue is indeed its own reward, and, besides, you can boast about finding him. The poor man of culture and the struggling artist live for one another, or at least they ought to—though I am afraid it is not much of a living for the struggling artist." He paused abruptly. "I suppose that autotype cost thirty shillings, and this carpet about five pounds?"

Bagshot assumed an elegant attitude against his bureau. He had discovered his reply. "You know you are bitten by the fashion for originality. Why should I make my room hideous with the work of third-rate mediocrity, or of men who are still learning to paint, simply in order to be unlike my neighbour?"

"Why," returned my uncle, "should you hang up things less interesting than your wall paper, in mere imitation of your neighbours? For this on your walls, Bagshot, deny it though you may, is not art but fashion. I tell you, you do not care a rap for art. You think pictures are a part of virtue, like a silk hat—or evening dress at dinner. And in your choice of

pictures you follow after your kind. I
never met a true-born Briton yet who
dared to buy a picture on his own accord
—unless he was a dealer. And then
usually he was not really a true-born
Briton. He waits to see what is being
hung. He has these things now because
he thinks they are right, not because they
are beautiful, just as he used to have the
Stag at Bay and the Boastful Hound. It
is Leighton now ; it was Landseer then.
Really I believe that very soon the ladies'
papers will devote a column to pictures.
Something in this style. 'Smart people
are taking down their Rossetti's Annun-
ciations now, and are hanging Gambier
Bolton's new Hippopotamus in the place
of it. This Hippopotamus is to be *the*
correct thing in pictures this year, and no
woman with any claim to be considered
smart will fail to have it over her piano.
Marcus Stone's new engraving will also be
rather *chic*. Watts's Hope is now considered a little dowdy.' And so forth.
This gregarious admiration is the very

antithesis of artistic appreciation, which I tell you, simply *must* be individual."

" Go on," said Bagshot, " go on."

" And that," said my uncle, with the glow of discovery in his face, " that is where the vulgar critic goes wrong. He conceives an orthodoxy. He tries to explain why Velasquez is better than Raphael and Raphael better than Gerard Dow. As well say why a cirrus cloud is better than a sycamore and a sycamore better than a scarlet hat. Every painter, unless he is a mere operative, must have his peculiar public. It is incredible that any painter can really satisfy the æsthetic needs of such a public as these reproductions indicate. True art is always sectarian. Why were Landseer and Sidney Cooper popular a few years ago, and why does every tea-table sneer at them now? There must be something admirable in them, or they would never have been admired. Then why has my niece Annie dropped admiring Poynter, and why does she pretend—and a very thin pretence it is—to admire Whistler ?"

" You are wandering from my pictures," said Bagshot.

" I want to," said my uncle. " But why do you try and hide your taste under these mere formalities in frames ? Why do you always say 'I pass' in the game of decoration ? Better a mess of green amateurs and love therewith, than the richest autotypes and dull complacency. Have what you like. There is no such thing as absolute beauty. That is the Magna Charta of the world of art. What is beautiful to me is not beautiful to another man, in art as in women. But take care to get the art that fits you. Frankly, that 'Love and Death' suits you, Bagshot, about as much as a purple toga would. Orchardson is in your style. I tell you that the greengrocer who buys an original oil painting for sixteen shillings with frame complete is far nearer artistic salvation than the patron of the popular autotype. Surely you will wake up presently, Bagshot, and wonder what you have been about.

"Half-past four, by Jove! I must be getting on. Well, Bagshot, ta-ta. One must talk, you know. I really hope you will be comfortable in your new rooms."

And so good-bye to Bagshot, staring in a puzzled way at his reviled and desecrated walls.

MY poor uncle came to me the other evening in a most distressful state, broken down to common blasphemy. His ample front was rumpled with sorrow and his tie disorderly aslant. His hair had gone rough with his troubles. "The time I have had, George!" he panted. "Give me something to drink in the name of Holy Charity."

Since the *Pall Mall Gazette* took to reporting his little sayings about photographs and ornaments, ideals and fashions, he has been setting up as a conversationalist. He thinks he was designed by Providence to that end, and aids his destiny as much as he can by elaborately preparing remarks.

Yet this thing had happened. "They put," said my uncle, "a little chap at the piano, and me at a very nice girl indeed as she looked ; and the little chap began, and so did I. I said a prelude thing of mine, brand new and rather pretty."

He stopped. He turned to nerve himself with whisky.

" Well," I said, when the pause seemed sufficient ; " what did she say ? "

My uncle looked unspeakable things. Then in a whisper, bending towards me :

" *She said——Sssh !* "

He repeated it that I might grasp its full enormity, " *Sssh !*—so ! "

" What *is* music," said my uncle, after a moody silence, "that reasonable people should listen to it ? I *had* to listen to it myself, and it struck me. It was just a tune this little chap was trying to remember, and now he would come at it this way and now that. He never got it quite right, though he fumbled about it for ten minutes or a quarter of an hour. And then two girls went, and one punished the piano while the other, with a wrist rather than an ear for music, drowned its cries with a violin. So it went on all the evening, and when I moved they all looked at me; I had been put on a nervous wicker chair, and I knew my shoes squeaked like a carnival of swine, and so I could not get away. And all the things that kept coming into my head, George, the neat remarks and graceful sayings !

" You see, I look at it in this light. Music is merely background, and ought to be kept in its place. I am no enemy of music, George. The air in a room should be melodious, for the same reason that it should be faintly pleasing to the olfactory sense, and neither hot nor stuffy. Just as the walls should be delightfully coloured and softly lit, and the refreshments pleasant and at the moment of need. But surely we meet for human intercourse. When I go to see people I go to see the people— not to hear a hired boy play the piano. But these people plant a *chevaux de frise* of singers and performers upon instruments of music between themselves and me.

They gag me with a few pennyworths of second-hand opera. There I was bursting to talk, and nice, intelligent-looking girls to talk to, and whenever I began to say something they said ' *Sssh !* ' Tantalus in a drawing-room it was — the very Hades of hospitality.

"Surely some day we shall learn refinement in our entertaining. Your modern hostess issues her invitations and seems overcome with consternation at her gathering. ' What *shall* I do with all these people ? ' she seems to ask. So she dabs cakes upon them, piles coffee cups over them : ' Eat,' she says, ' and shut up ! ' and stifles their protests with a clamorous woman and a painful piano.

" No, of course I don't object to having music. But it is an accessory, not an object, in life. It is, after all, a physical comfort, a pleasant vibration in one's ears. To make an object of it is sensuality. It is on all-fours with worshipping the wall-paper. Some wall-papers are very beautiful things nowadays, harmonious in form and colour, skilful in invention ; but people do not expect you to sit down and admire wall-paper, or promise you ' wall-paper at eight.' Neither do they put an extinguisher over any girl who does not go with the wall-paper, or expect you to dress in neutral tint on account of it, and they are not hurt if you go away without seeming to see it. Gustatory harmony, too, is · very delicious. Yet there is no hush during dinner ; they do not insist upon a persistent gnawing in honour of the feast. But these musical people ! their god is their piano. They set up an idol in their salon, and command all the world to bow down to it. They found a priestcraft of pianists, and an Inquisition of fiddlers. When I came away they were all crowded round a violin, the women especially. They could not have fussed more if it had been a baby. They stroked it and admired its figure. It *had* rather a fashionable figure, but the neck was too long. . . ."

I began to suspect the cause of this bitterness.

" Yes. She *was* there. And while some of this piano was going on she looked at the ear of the man who was playing with a dreamy, tender look. . . . No. I couldn't get a word with her the whole evening."

As I was passing the London University
the other day I saw my uncle emerge
from the branch of the Bank of England ⁻
opposite, and proceed in the direction of
the Burlington Arcade. He was elaborately disguised as a young man, even to
the youthful flower, and I was incontinently
smitten with curiosity respecting the dark
purpose he might veil in this way.   There
is, to me, a peculiar and possibly rather a
childish fascination in watching my more
intimate friends unobserved, and, curiously
enough, I had never before studied the
avuncular back view. I found something
singularly entertaining in the study of the
graceful contour of his new frock coat, and
in the cheerful carriage of his cane. He
paraded, a dignified procession of one,
some way down the Arcade, hesitated for

48

a moment outside a jeweller's shop, and then entered it. I strolled on as far as Piccadilly, returned to the shop, and so fell upon him suddenly in the midst of his buying.

"Hullo, George!" he said hastily, facing me so as to hide as much of the counter as possible. "How's Euphemia?"

I looked him fairly in the eye. "You are buying a *ring*," I said in a firm, decided voice.

He turned to the counter with an air of surprise. "By Jove, so I am!"

"A lady's ring," I said. He was, I could see, hastily collecting his sufficiently nimble powers of subterfuge. "One must buy something, you know, George, sometimes," he said feebly.

He had selected some dozen or so already, the most palpable engagement rings I think I ever saw. One of them had visible on its inner curvature the four letters MIZP—. He looked at them, saw the posy, and then, glancing at me, laughed affably. "I meant to tell you

D

yesterday, George—I will take these," to the shopman. And we emerged with a superficial amiability ; the case of rings in my uncle's pocket. The thing was rather a shock to me, coming so suddenly and unexpectedly. I had anticipated some innocent purchase of the jewellery he reviles so much, but certainly not significant rings, golden fetters for others to wear and enslave him ; and we were past the flower-shop towards Hyde Park before either of us spoke. It seemed so dreadful to me that the cheerful, talkative man beside me, my own father's little brother, a traveller in distant countries, and a most innocent man, and with all the inveterate habits of thirty years' honourable bachelorhood and all the mellowness of life upon him, should, without consulting me, have taken the first irrevocable step towards becoming a ratepayer, a pew tenant, paterfamilias, a fighter with schoolmasters, and the serf of a butler, that I scarcely knew what to say adequate to the occasion.

"Well," said I at last, with an in-

voluntary sigh, " I suppose I must congratulate you."

" Don't look at it in that light, George,"
said my uncle; and he added in a more
cheerful tone, " I am only going to get
engaged, you know."

" You can scarcely imagine, George,"
he proceeded, " how I have longed to be
engaged. All my life it has been my
hope and goal. It is, I think, tħe ideal
state of man. There was a chap with me
when I was at Kimberley who first put
the idea into my head. His ways were
animated and cheerful even for a diamond
field, where you know animation and
cheerfulness are, so to speak, *de rigueur*.
Whisky he affected, and jesting of the
kind that paints cities scarlet. And he
used every night, before festivities began,
to write a long letter to some girl in
England, and say, within limits, how bad
he had been and how he longed to reform
and be with her, and never, never do
anything wrong any more. He poured
all the higher and better parts of his

nature into the letter, and folded it up
and sealed it very carefully. And then
he came to us in a singularly relieved
frame of mind, and would be the life and
soul of as merry a game of follow-your-
leader as one can well imagine."

Pleasant reminiscences occupied him for
a moment. "Every man should be engaged, I think, to at least one woman. It
is the homage we owe to womankind, and
a duty to our souls. His *fiancée* is indeed
the Madonna of a true-hearted man ; the
thought of her is a shrine at the wayside
of one's meditations, and her presence a
temple wherein we cleanse our souls. She
is mysterious, worshipful, and inaccessible,
something perhaps of the woman, possibly
even propitious and helpful, and yet something of the Holy Grail as well. You
have no rights with her, nor she with you ;
you owe her no definite duties, and yet
she is singularly yours. A smile is a
favour, a touch of her fingers, a faint pressure of your hand, is an infinite privilege.
You cannot demand the slightest help or

concern of her, so you ask it with diffident grace and there is an everflowing stream of gratitude from small occasions. Whatever you give her is a gift too, while a husband is just property, a mere draught-camel for her service. All your functions are decorative, you hang her shrine with flowers and precious stones. You treat her to art and literature, and as for vulgar necessities—some one else sees to that."

" Until you are married," began I.

" I am speaking of being engaged. Marriage is altogether a different thing. The essence of a proper engagement is reverence, distance, and mystery; the essence of marriage is familiarity. A *fiancée* is a living eidolon; a wife, from my point of view at least, should be a confidential companion, a fellow-conspirator, an accessory after the fact, at least, to one's little errors; should take some share of the burthen and heat of the day with one, and have the humour to bear with a mood of vexation or a fit of the blues. I doubt, do you know, if the same kind of girl is

suitable for engagements as for marriage.
For an engagement give me something
very innocent, a little awe-inspiring on
that account, absolutely and tenderly worshipful, yet given to moods of caressing affec-
tion, and altogether graceful and beautiful.
A man, I think, ought to be incapable of
smoking or lounging in front of the girl he
professes to love, so reverent ought his love
to be.   But for marriage let me have humour
and some community of taste, a woman
who can climb stiles and stand tobacco
smoke, and who knows a good cook by her
fruits. . . .   It is a complicated business,
this marrying.

"The familiarity of the marriage state,
if it does not breed positive contempt on
the part of the angel, engenders at times,
I think, a considerable craving for change
on the side of both parties.   We men are
poor creatures at the best—I always pity
your Euphemia.   Married people, for
instance, always get too much of each
other's conversation.   They do not have
sufficient opportunity to recuperate their

topics from original sources. They get interested in outside people, merely from a perfectly legitimate desire to get some amusing novel ideas for each other, and then comes jealousy. I sometimes think that if Adam and Eve had been merely engaged, she would not have talked with the serpent; and the world had been saved an infinity of misery.

"No, George: engagements for me. It is the state we were made for. I have delayed this matter all too long. But, thank heaven, I am engaged at last—I hope for all the rest of my life. Now, will you not congratulate me?"

"It may be very nice as you put it, but engagements end as well as begin," I insisted. "You cannot be a law unto yourself in these matters. When will you get married?"

"Good Heavens!" exclaimed my uncle. "Get married and end this delightful state! You don't think she will want me to marry her, do you? Besides, she told me some time ago that she did not intend to marry

again.   It was only that encouraged me to
suggest an engagement to her.   Though
she is a wonderful woman, George—a
wonderful woman.   Still, I think she looks
at things very much as I do."

He paused thoughtfully.   Then added
with fervour, " At least I hope so."

LA BELLE DAME SANS MERCI

A RHAPSODY

I FOUND him in his own apartments, and strangely disordered. He went to and fro, raving—beginning so soon as I entered the room. I noticed a book half out of its cover, flung carelessly into the corner of the room.

" I am enchanted of an impalpable woman, George," he said, " I am in bonds to a spirit of the air. I can neither think nor work nor eat nor sleep because of her. Sometimes I go out suddenly, tramping through seething streets, through fog and drizzle or dry east wind, mourning for her sake. My life is rapidly becoming one colourless melancholy through her spells and twining sorceries. I sometimes wish that I were dead.

57

" Yet I have never seen her.   Often, indeed, I imagine her, anon as of this shape, and anon of that.   I know her only by her victims, those she slays daily, and daily revives to slay.   They come to me with their complaints, mutilated, pathetic, terrible.   I try to shut my ears to them in vain.   I have tried wool, but it made little or no difference.

" The business always begins with the slamming of a door and a healthy footfall across the room.   The piano is opened. Then some occasional noises—the falling of a piece of music behind the piano, perhaps, and its extraction by means of the tongs—I know it is tongs she uses by the clang.   Then the music-stool creaks, and La Belle Dame is ready to play.   She puts both her hands upon the key-board, and the treble shrieks apprehensively, and the bass roars like a city in revolt.   After that this hush.   Just this interval.

" Yet I sometimes think this hush is really the worst of it all.   It is a volumin- ous apprehension, a towering impendency.

You don't understand, George. You can't. The poor devil in Poe's 'Pit and the Pendulum' must have had a taste of my sensations. A first victim is being chosen. I have a vision of the spirits of composers small and great—standing up like suspects awaiting identification, while her eye ranges over them. Chopin tries to edge behind Wagner, a difficult and forbidding person, and Gounod seeks eclipse of Mendelssohn, who suddenly drops and crawls on all fours between Gounod's legs; Sullivan cowers, and even Piccolomini's iron-framed nerves desert him. She extends her hand. There is a frantic rush to escape. Have you ever seen a little boy picking dormice out of a cage? I always see this same nightmare during that dreadful pause, a vision of a writhing heap of kicking, struggling, maddened composers, and of a ghoulish piano grinning expectant, jaw raised—lid I mean—and showing all its black and yellow keys. . . . A melancholy shriek. Do you hear, George? Tito Mattei is captured. A song.

" ' Pum—So long the way—Pum—so
dark the day — Pum — DEAR HEART !
before you come.' So Tito Mattei comes
pumming through the wall into my presence. I don't pity him. Indeed it is a
positive relief that it is only Tito Mattei.
The man's no deity at the best, and a
little pulling out, and pulling crooked, and
general patching together of limbs in the
wrong place scarcely matters so far as he
and my taste are concerned. Yet I always
leave my work, George, when that begins,
and walk about the room. I try to per-
suade myself that I need fresh air, but the
autumnal day, the damp shiny street, has
all the uninviting harshness of truth—I
admit I do not. Tito flops about, is
riddled with dropped notes and racked
with hesitations, and presently becomes
still. The murder is over.

" What next ? That Study of Chopin's !
This time the thing is more inspiring.
Once upon a time it was a favourite of
mine. Now it is a favourite of the un-
seen lady's. She plays it with spirit,

and conjures up strange fancies in my brain. The noises that come through the wall now, quicker, thicker, louder, are full of a tale of weltering confusion, marine disaster, a ship in sore labour ; there is a steady beating like the sound of pumps, and a trickle of treble notes. There are black silences, like thunderclouds, that burst into flashes of music. Now the poor melody swings up into the air— then comes one of those terrible pauses, and now down into the abyss. A crash, an ineffectual beating, a spasmodic rush. I seem to hear the pumps again, distant, remote, ineffectual. But that is not so ; the struggle is over. Chopin's Study has been battered to pieces ; only disarticulated fragments toss amidst the froth. High up the confusion of the stormy sky she drives in a sieve dropping notes— the witch of the storm, La Belle Dame Sans Merci.

"But the third piece in her repertory has begun—Rubinstein. This, at any rate, is familiar. She plays with the

confidence born of long unpunished mis-
doing.   That Rubinstein must indeed be
sorry, and unless their elysium is like the
library of the Linnæan Society, and fitted
with double windows, all the great departed musicians must be sorry too, that
he ever wrote a Melody in F.   Daily
from the altars of a thousand, of ten
thousand, school pianos that melody cries
to heaven.   From the empire of the
music master, upon which the sun never
sets, day and night, week in week out,
from year to year, Rubinstein's Melody
in F streams up for ever.   These school
pieces are like the Latin ritual before the
Reformation, they link all Christendom
by a common use.   As the earth spins,
and the sunlight sweeps ever westward,
that melody passes with the day.   Now
it is tinkling in a grey Moravian school,
now it dawns upon the Adige and begins
in Alsace, now it has reached Madrid,
Paris, London.   Then a devotee in some
Connemara   Establishment   for   Young
Ladies sets to.   Presently tall ships upon

the silent main resound with it, and
they are at it in the Azores and in
Iceland, and then—one solitary tinkling,
doubling, reduplicating, manifolding into
an innumerable multitude—New York
takes up the wondrous tale.   On then
with the dawn to desolate cattle ranches,
the tablelands of Mexico, the level plains
of Illinois and Michigan.   So the great
tide that started in Rubinstein's cranium
proceeds upon its destiny.   Always somewhere between the hours of eleven and
two it comes back to me here, poor
hunted composition, running its eternal
world gauntlet, pursuing its Wandering
Jew pilgrimage, and I curse and pity it
as it goes by. . . . It has gone.   The
' Maiden's Prayer ' is next usually.   Then
one of the ' Lieder ohne Worte,' then the
' Dead March '—all of them ᴠbut the
meagre and mutilated skeletons of themselves; things of gaps and tatters, like
gibbet trophies.   They are as knocked
about as a fleet coming out of action,
they are as twisted and garbled as a

Chinese war telegram ; it is like an hospital for congenitally diseased compositions taking the air. And they have to hobble along sharply too ; there is a certain cruel decision in the way the notes are struck, a Nurse Gillespie touch about this Invisible Lady. Or it may be the callousness of old habit, a certain sense of a duty overdone, a certain im-. patience at the long delay. You will hear.

" Listen ! — *Tum Tum Ti-ti-tum* — No !—*tum*. Slight pause. *Tum tum twiddle*—vigorous crescendo—TUM. This is unusual ! A stranger ? A new piece for La Belle Dame Sans Merci ? Her wonted reckless dash deserts her. She is, as it were, exploring a new region, and advances with mischievous coyness, with an affectation of a faltering heart, with hesitating steps. My imagination is stimulated by these dripping notes. I see her, as it were, on an uneven pavement ; here the flags are set on end, there fungi have tilted them, a sharp turning of the page may reveal heaven knows what horrors; presently comes a black gap with a vault of dusty silence below. A pause, an incoherency, a re-petition! She has encountered some difficulty, some slumbering coil of sharps and flats, and it raises its bristling front in her way. . . . She has fled back to the opening again. I begin to wonder what unhappy musician lies hidden in this new ruin, behind the bars of this melancholy confusion. There is some-thing familiar but elusive, like a face that one has known and loved and lost and met again after the cruel changes of intervening years. It conjures up oddly enough a vision of a long room in the twilight, and an acacia in silhouette against the pale gold of the western sky. Ah! now I know!

" *That* of all pieces!

" I must have my walk, George. I can-not bear to hear that old-familiar music so evilly entreated. But, all the same, the memory it has touched will vibrate and smart; to-day and to-morrow, and

E

I know not for how many days, it will
re-echo in my brain. All the old cloudy
remorse that has subsided will be set
astir again. I shall hear again a light
touch upon the keys, see again the
shadowy face against the sunset, try to
recall the sound of a voice. . . . What
evil spirit has put this mockery into the
head of La Belle Dame? Surely without
this———"

He made a dive at the folding doors
and presently reappeared in his coat. It
was the only intimation I ever had that
my dear little uncle had such a thing
as a Past.

ON A TRICYCLE

I SAT on the parapet of the bridge, and swung my feet over the water that frothed and fretted at the central pier below. Above the bridge the stream broadened into a cress-bespangled pool, over which the sapphire dragon-flies hovered, and its earlier course was hidden by the big oak trees that bent towards each other from either bank. Through their speckled tracery of green one saw the hazy blue depths of the further forest. I was watching the proceedings of some quick-moving brown bird amid the rushes and marsh marigolds of the opposite bank.

"Pleasant," said a voice beside me.

I turned, and saw my uncle. He was disguised in a costume of reddish-brown cloth. "Golf here?" said I, and then I noticed the tricycle. "A vagrom man on wheels!"

Both the suit and the machine became him very well. The machine was low, and singularly broad between the wheels, and altogether equal to him, and it had chubby pneumatic tires and a broad and even imposing wallet.

"Yes," said he, following my eye. "It is a handsome machine, a full dress concern with all its plating and brown leathei, and in use it is as willing and quiet as any tricycle could be, a most urbane and gentlemanly affair—if you will pardon the adjective. I am glad these things have not come too late for me. Frankly, the bicycle is altogether too flippant for a man of my age, and the tricycle hitherto, with its two larger wheels behind and a smaller one in front, has been so indecently suggestive of a perambulator that really, George, I could not bring myself to it. But a Bishop might ride *that* thing."

He swung himself up upon the parapet beside me and lit a cigar.

"The bicycle for boys, George—or fools. The things will not keep up for a moment without you work at them, they need constant attention ; I would as soon ride a treadmill. You cannot loaf with them, and the only true pleasure of cycling is to loaf. Yet only this morning did I meet an elderly gentleman with a beard fit for Abraham, his face all crimson and deliquescent with heat, and all distorted with the fury of his haste, toiling up a hill on one of these unstable instruments. When he saw me coming down in all my ease and dignity he damned at me with his bell. Now, I do not like to see a bicycle wobble under a load of years, and steer into the irascible. As years increase tempers shorten, and bicycles, even the best of bicycles, are seductively irritating.

"Besides, the devil of the Wandering Jew has power over all such as go upon two wheels. 'Onward,' he says, ' onward ! Faster, thou man ! This green and breezy earth is no abiding place for you !' And hard-breathing, crook-shaped, whirling, bell-banging lunatics try and race you. They whiz by, thinking indignities of your dignified progress, and sometimes saying them. Not one cyclist in a dozen, George, and seemingly not a solitary bicyclist, seems to think of anything but getting to the end of his pleasure. I meet these servants of the wheel at the inns, and they tell short stories and sketches about their pace, and show each other their shoes and saddles, and compare maps and roads; some even try to trade machines. They talk most indecently of the makes and prices. I would as soon ask a man who was his tailor or where he got his hair cut and how much he paid. One man I met was not so much a man as a hoarding, blatant about the Gaspipe Machine Company. For them no flowers exist, no wild birds, no trees, no landscapes, no historical memorials, and no geological associations, nothing but the roads they traverse and the bicycles they ride. Those that have other interests have them in the form of cheap portable cameras, malignant things that can find no beauty in earth or heaven."

" George," said my uncle, suddenly, and I knew he had come upon a great discovery ; " real human beings are scarce in this world."

" You speak bitterly," said I. " I know what has happened. You are hot from an inn full of the viler type of cyclist, and I presume that, after their custom, they mocked at your machinery. But don't blacken a popular exercise on that account."

" But these men are so aggressive ! I tell you, George, it requires moral courage to ride a tricycle about at a moderate pace, as a man of discretion should. They want to make a sport of it ; they are race-struck, incapable of understanding a man who rides at seven miles an hour when he might ride at fifteen. Read their special papers. They mock and sneer at everything but pace ; they worship the makes of '94 in the interests of their advertising columns ; touring simply means hotel-touting to them, and landscape, deals in cameras ; in the end they will kill cycling—indeed, they are killing it. It is not nice to be

mocked at even when you are in the right ;
a blatant cad is like a rhinoceros, and
admits of no parleying, only since you must
not kill him you are obliged to keep out
of his way.   The common cyclist has
already driven ladies off the roads by
forcing the pace, the honeymoon tandem
returns with its feelings hurt at his jesting,
and now he is driving off all quiet men."

" All this," said I, " because they said
something disrespectful about your machine
at the last inn . . . You don't, I see,
approve of the feminine bicycle ? "

My uncle did his best to be calm and
judicial.

" A woman in a hurry is one of the
most painful sights in the world, for exertion does not become a woman as it does
a man.   Let us avoid all prejudice in this
matter, George, and discuss it with open
minds.   She has, in the first place, a
considerable length of hair, and she does
it up into rich and beautiful shapes with
things called hairpins and with curling
irons.   Very few people have hair that

curls naturally, George. You are young, but you are married, and I see nothing improper in telling you these things. Well, when a woman rides about, exerting herself violently to keep a bicycle going, her hair gets damp and the pleasing curls lose their curliness and become wet, straggling bands of hair plastered over her venous forehead. And a tragic anxiety is manifest, an expression painful for a man to meet. Also her hairpins come out and fall on the road to wait for pneumatic tires, and her hair is no longer rich and beautiful in form. Then she gets dirty, horribly dirty, as though she had been used to sweep the roads with. And her skirts have to be weirdly altered, even to the divided skirt, so that when she rides she looks like a short, squat little man. She not only loses her beauty but her dignity. Now, for my own part, I think a man wants a woman to worship—it is a man's point of view, of course, but I can't help my sex—and the worshipping of these zouaves is incredible. She is nothing more than a shorter, fuller, and feebler man. Heaven help her ! For the woman on the tricycle there are ampler excuses as well as ampler skirts, the exertion is not too violent for grace and coolness, and the offensive bulging above one narrow wheel is avoided. But women will never sacrifice so much for so little ; worshipfulness, beauty, repose, and comfort for a paltry two or three miles more an hour of pace. They know too well the graces of delay. To do things slowly, George, is part of the art of living. Our sex learns that when its youthful fervour is over and all the things are done. But women are born wise."

" By the bye," said I, " how is Mrs Harborough ? "

" Very well, thanks. How is Euphemia ? Your bit of view, George, is pretty, but I think I will have some heather now. There is a common three miles ahead. This indeed is the true merit of cycling. For a view, a panorama ; for one picture, a gallery. Your true artist in cycling sits by the roadside, and rides only by way of an interlude. As for the worship of the machine, I would as soon worship a scene-shifter."

He dropped off the bridge and mounted his machine, and was presently pursuing his smooth and noiseless way. As he vanished round the corner he sounded his gong. It was really a most potent, grave, and reverend gong, with a certain note of philosophical melancholy in its tone, as different from the vulgar tang of your common cycle as one can well imagine. It asked you, at your convenience, sir (or madam), to get out of the way, to stand aside and see a most worthy and dignified spectacle roll by, if so be you had the mind for it. As for any scolding insistence, any threat of imminent collision, there was none of it. It was the bell of a man who loved margins, who was at his ease, and would have all the world at its ease. More than anything else, it reminded me of the boom of some ivy-clad church tower, warning the world without unseemly haste that another hour had, with leisurely completeness, accomplished itself.

And so he passed out of my sight and was gone.

AN UNSUSPECTED MASTERPIECE

(AUTHORESS UNKNOWN)

HE pushed it away from him.

"I felt as though I had disturbed the graves of the long departed," he said with a grimace, and then addressing the egg: "Forgive me the sacrilege: they sold you to me as new laid, a mere thing of yesterday. I had no idea I was opening the immemorial past. *De mortuis nihil nisi bonum*—to *you* at least the quotation will be novel. Or I might call you bad, you poor mummy.

"Unhappy, pent-up, ineffectual thing!" he said, waving his jilted bread and butter, and addressing the discarded inedible. "Poor old maid among eggs! And so it has come to this absolute failure with you. Why were you ever laid? Surely,

77

since you were once alive, some lurking
aspiration, some lowly, and yet not lowly,
but most divine, striving towards the
Higher and the Better, hath stirred within
you. The warm sunlight shone through
your translucent shell, the sweet air
stirred the sweet hay of the nest, and
life called you from your dreaming to
awake, and join it in its interplay. And
now! You might have been — what
might you not have been? A prize
hen, fountain of a broadening stream of
hens, chicks, dozens of chicks, hundreds
of chicks, a surging ocean of chickens.
Had you been hatched among the early
Victorian chickens that were, I presume,
your contemporaries, by now you might
have been a million fowl, and the delight
and support of hundreds of thousands of
homes. You might have been worth
thousands of pounds and have eaten corn
by the ton. They might have written
articles about you in half-crown reviews
and devoted poultry farms to your sole
support. And instead you have been

narrowed down to this sordid back-street tragedy, a mere offence, tempting a struggling tradesman to risk the honour of my patronage of his books, for a paltry fraction of a pennyworth of profit. Why, I ask you, were you not hatched? Was it lack of courage? a fear of the unknown dangers that lie outside the shell?

"An indescribable pity wells up in me for this lost egg, this dead end in the tree of life, George. One thinks of the humble but deserving amœba, the primordial metazöon, the first fish, the remote reptile ancestor, the countless generations of forefathers that, so far as this egg went, have lived and learnt and suffered in vain. The torrent of life had split and rushed by on either side of it. And you might," cried he, turning to the egg again, "have been a Variety, a novelty, and an improvement in chickens. No chick now will ever be *exactly* the chick you might have been. Only an Olive Schreiner could do full justice to your failure, you poor nun, you futile eremite, you absolute and hopeless *impasse*. Was it, I ask again, a lack of courage ?

" Perhaps a lack of opportunity ? It may be you stirred and hoped in the distant past, and the warmth to quicken you never came. Ambition may have fretted you. Indeed, now I think of it, there is something in the flavour of you, singularly suggestive of disappointed ambi-tion. In literature, and more particularly in criticism, I can assure you I have met the very fellow of your quality, from literary rotten eggs whose opening came too late. They are like the genii in the ' Arabian Nights ' whom Solomon, the son of David, sealed in the pot. At first he promised infinite delights to his discoverer —and his discoverer lagged. In the end he was filled with unreasonable hatred against all the feeble free, and emerged as a malignant fume, eager to wreak him-self upon the world.

" A sudden thought, George ! I see my egg in a new light, and all my pity changes to respect. Surely it is a most potent egg, a gallinaceous Swift.   After all, anything but pointless and childless, since it has this strange quality of being offensive and engendering thought.   Food for the mind if not food for the body— didactic if not delightful—a bit of modern literature, earnest and fundamentally real. I must try and understand you, Ibsen Ovarum.   Possibly it is a profound parable I have stumbled upon.   Though I scarcely reckoned on a parable with my bread and butter.   Frankly, I must confess I bought it for the eating."

Now that my uncle had at last begun to grasp the true greatness of his egg, he apparently considered it becoming to drop the tone of half-patronising pity he had previously adopted.   " Come," said he, smiling, with a dash of raillery, over his coffee-cup ; " admit you are a humbug, you whitened sepulchre of an anticipated chick !   Until you found a congenial soul and overwhelmed me with your confidence, what a career of deception—not mean, of course, but cynical—ironical—you have been leading. What a jest it must have been to you to be sold as new laid! How you laughed in your quiet way at the mockery of life. Surely it was a worthy pair to Swift in cassock and bands conducting a marriage service. I can well fancy your silent scorn of the hand that put you in the bag. New laid! But now I have the full humour of you. You must pardon my dulness of apprehension. I grasp your meaning now; your quiet insistent teaching that all life is decay and all decay is life. No forcing the accent, no crudity, but a pervading persuasion. A noble gospel!"

He paused impressively, placed the egg respectfully upon his bureau, and presently went off at a tangent to something else.

"Shall I throw this away?" said the girl.

"Good heavens! Throw it away? Certainly not. Put it in the library." (The library used to be the corner of the room by the window.)

She stared at me with a certain attempt at confidence. She is a callous, impertinent kind of girl, and I fear inclined to be bold. "It *do* smell, sir," she said to him.

"That's the merit of it. It's irony. Go and put it on the fourth shelf near the window. There are some yellow-covered books there, and Swift, some comedies by a gentleman named Ibsen, and a couple of novels by two gentlemen named George ——. But there! you don't know one book from another! The fourth shelf from the top on the right-hand side."

As the girl did so she looked over her hand at me, and lifted her eyebrows very slightly.

MY uncle had been hectic all day. I knew and dreaded what was coming, and said nothing that by any chance could lead up to it.

He absent-mindedly tipped the emu sixpence. Then we came to the wart hog.

"A bachelor," he said, meditatively, scratching the brute's back.

I hastily felt for a saving topic in the apprehensive darkness of my mind, and could find none.

"I expect I shall be married in October," said my uncle. Then, sighing: "The idyll of my engagement was short-lived."

It was out. Now, the day—my last idle day with my poor uncle—was a hideous wreck. All the topics he had fluttered round vanished, and, cold and awful, there loomed over us the one great topic.

"What do you *think* of marriage, George?" said my uncle, after a pause, prodding the wart hog suddenly.

"That's your privilege," said I. "Married men don't dare to think of it. Bigamy."

"Privilege! Is it such a headlong wreck of one's ideals as they say?" said my uncle. "Is that dreamland furniture really so unstable in use?"

"Of course," said I, "it's different from what one expects. But it seems to be worse for the other party. At least to judge from the novels they engender in their agony."

"So far as I can see," he proceeded, "what happens is very similar to a thing a scientific chap was explaining to me the other day. There are some little beasts in the sea called ascidians, and they begin life as cheerful little tadpole things, with waggling tails and big expressive eyes.

They move freely about hither and thither, and often travel vast distances in an adventurous way.   Then what he called metamorphosis begins.   The little tadpole waggles his way to a rock and fixes himself head downward.   Then he undergoes the oddest changes, becomes indeed a mere vegetative excrescence on the stone, secretes a lot of tough muck round himself, and is altogether lost to free oceanic society.   He loses the cheerful tail, loses most of his brain, loses his bright expressive eye."

"The bother of it," said I, "is that very often the wandering expressive eye is not lost in the human metamorphosis."

"Putting it in another way, one might say that the kind of story that Ovid is so fond of describing, the affairs of Daphne and Io, for instance, are fables of the same thing : an interlude of sentiment and then a change into something new and domesticated, rooted, fixed, and bounded in."

"It is certainly always a settling down," said I.

"I don't like this idea of settling down,

George." He shuddered. "It must be a dreadful thing to go about always with a house on your mind."

"You get used to it. And, besides, you don't go about so much."

He gave the bachelor wart hog a parting dig, and we walked slowly and silently through the zebra-house towards the elephants. "Of course *we* do not intend to settle down," he said presently, with a clumsy effort to render his previous remarks impersonal.

"A marriage invalidates all promises," I explained. "The law recognises this in the case of wills."

"That's a new view," he said, evidently uncomfortable about something.

"It follows from your doctrine of metamorphosis. A marries B. Then the great change begins. A gradually alters into a new fixed form, C, while B flattens and broadens out as D. It is a different couple, and they cannot reasonably be held responsible for the vagaries of A and B."

" That ought to be better understood."

" It would perhaps be as well. Before marriage Edwin vows to devote his life to Angelina, and Angelina vows she will devote her life to Edwin. After marriage this leads to confusion if they continue to believe such promises. Marriage certainly has that odd effect on the memory. You remember Angelina's promises and forget your own, and *vice versa*."

" There is no apparition more distressing than the ghost of a dead promise," said my uncle. " Especially when it is raised in the house of your friends."

We passed through the elephant house in silence.

"I wonder what kind of man I shall be after the change, George. It's all a toss-up," he continued, after an interval. "I have seen some men improved by it. You, for instance. You were a mere useless, indecent aspirant to genius before the thing came upon you. Now you are a respectable journalist and gracefully anxious to give satisfaction to your editor.

But my own impression is that a man has to be a bit of an ass before he can be improved by marriage. Most men get so mercenary, they simply work and do nothing a rational creature should. They are like the male ants that shed their wings after the nuptial flight. And their wives go round talking fashion articles, and calling them dear old stupids, and flirting over teacups with the unmarried men, or writing novelettes about the child-man, and living their own lives. I've been an unmarried man and I know all about it. Every intelligent woman now seems to want to live her own life when she is not engaged in taking the child-man out into polite society, and trying to wean him from alcohol and tobacco. However, this scarcely applies to me."

" Not now," I said. And he winced.

" I wonder how it feels. Most men go into this without knowing of the change that hangs over them. But I am older. It would not be nice for a cater-pillar if he knew he was going to rip up all along his back in a minute or so. Yet I could sympathise with such a cater-pillar now. Anyhow, George, I hope the change will be complete. I would not like to undergo only a partial metamor-phosis, and become a queer speckled monster all spotted with bachelor habits. Yet I sometimes think I am beyond the adolescent stage, and my habits rather deeply rooted. Hitherto, I have always damned a little at braces and collars and things like that. · I wish I knew where one could pick up a few admissible expletives. And I loaf about London all day sometimes without any very clear idea of what I am after, telling chaps in studios how to paint, and talk-ing to leisurely barristers, and all that kind of thing."

" *She*," I said, "will probably help you to conquer habits of that sort."

"Yes, I dare say she will," said my uncle. "I forgot that for the minute."

THE PAINS OF MARRIAGE

MY uncle came to a stop outside a stationer's shop in Oxford-street. When I saw what had caught his attention I reproached myself for my thoughtlessness.

"Come," said I, "tell me what you think of—of representative government."

"It's no good, George. You did the same thing at the cake shop. Do you think I never saw the cake shop? Since this affair was settled I think every shop I pass reminds me of it—even the gunsmith's. I never suspected before how entirely retail trade turned on marriage—except, perhaps, the second-hand book shops. The whole world seems a-marrying.

"It's queer," said he, "that a little while ago the thing that worried me to the exclusion of everything else was the idea of being married, and now it is so

near it's entirely the getting married that
upsets me. I have forgotten the horrid
consequences in the horror of the operation."

" It's much the same," said I, "at an
execution."

" Look at those cards." He waved his
hand towards a neat array of silver and
white pasteboard. " ' Jemima Smith,' with
an arrow through the Smith, and ' Podger '
written above it, and on the opposite
side ' Mr and Mrs John Podger.' That
is where it has me, George."

We went on past a display of electro-
plate with a card about presents in the
window, past a window full of white flowers,
past a carriage-builder's and a glove shop.
" It's like death," said my uncle; "it
turns up everywhere and is just the same
for everybody. In that cake shop there
were piles and piles of cakes, from little
cakes ten inches across up to cakes of
three hundredweight or so; all just the
same rich, uneatable, greasy stuff, and with
just the same white sugar on the top of
them. I suppose every day they pack off

scores. It makes one think of marrying
in swarms, like the gnats. I catch myself
wondering sometimes if the run of people
really are separate individuals, or only
a kind of replicas, without any tastes of
their own. There are people who would
rather not marry than marry without one
of those cakes, George. To me it seems
to be almost the most asinine position
a couple of adults can be in, to have to
buy a stone or so of that concentrated
biliousness and cut it up, or procure other
people to cut it up, and send it round to
other adults who would almost as soon eat
arsenic. And why cake—infantile cake?
Why not biscuits, or cigarettes, or choco-
late? It seems to me to be playing the
fool with a solemn occasion."

"You see, it is the custom to have cake."

"Well, anyhow, I intend to break the
custom."

"So did I, but I had it all the same."

My uncle looked at me.

"You see," said I, "when a woman
says you *must* do this or that—must have

cake at a wedding, for instance—you must
do it. It is not a case for argument. It
is a kind of privilege they have — the
categorical imperative. You will soon
learn that."

Evidently the question was open. "But
why do they say you must?"

"Other women tell them to. They
would 'despise any one dreadfully who did
not have a really big cake—from that
shop."

"But why?"

"My dear uncle," said I, "you are
going into matrimony. You do not show
a proper spirit."

"The cake," said my uncle, "is only a
type. There is this trousseau business
again. Why should a woman who is
going to marry require a complete outfit
of that sort? It seems to suggest—well,
pre-nuptial rags at least, George. Then
the costume. Why should a sane healthy
woman be covered up in white gauze like
the confectionery in a shop window when
the flies are about? And why—— ?"

He was going on in quite an aggressive tone. " There isn't a *why*," I said, " for any of it." This sort of talk always irritates a married man because it revives his own troubles. " It's just the rule. Surely, if a wife is worth having she is worth being ridiculous for ? You ought to be jolly glad you don't have to wear a fool's cap and paint your nose red. ' More precious than rubies '——"

" Don't," he said.

" It must be these tradesmen," he began bitterly after an interval. " Some one must be responsible, and it's just their way. Do you know, George, I sometimes fancy that they have hypnotised womankind into the belief that all these uncomfortable things are absolutely necessary to a valid marriage—just as they have persuaded the landlady class that no house is complete without a big mirror over the fireplace and a bulgy sideboard. There is a very strong flavour of mesmeric suggestion about a woman's attitude towards these matters, considered in the light of her customary common sense.   Do you know, George, I really believe there is a secret society of tradesmen, a kind of priesthood, who get hold of our womenkind and muddle them up with all these fancies.   It's a sort of white magic.   Have you ever been in a draper's shop, George ? "

" Never," I said : " I always wait out-side—among the dogs."

" Have you ever read a ladies' news-paper ? "

" I didn't know," said I, " that there was any part to read.   It's all advertise-ments ; all the articles are advertisements, all the paragraphs, the stories, the answers to correspondents—everything."

" That's exactly what makes me think the tradesmen have hypnotised the sex. It may be they do it in those drapers' dens. A man spots that kind of thing at once and drops the paper.   Women go on year after year, simply worshipping a paper hoarding of that kind, and doing patiently everything they are told to do therein. Anyhow, it is only in this way that I can account for all these expensive miseries of matrimony. I can't understand a woman in full possession of her faculties deliberately exasperating the man she has to live with — I suppose all men submit to it under protest — for these stale and stereotyped antics. She *must* be magnetised."

"They are not stale to her," I said.

"Mrs Harborough——" he began.

"Of course, a widow !—I forgot," I said. "But she seems so young, you know."

"And putting aside the details," said my uncle, with a transient dash of cheerfulness at my mistake; "I object to the publicity of the whole thing. It's not nice. To bring the street arab into the affair, to subject yourself to the impertinent congratulations and presents of every aspirant to your intimacy, to be patted on the back in the local newspapers as though you were going to do something clever. Confound them ! It's not their affair. And I'm too old to be a blushing bridegroom. Then think, what am I to do,

George, if that cad Hagshot sends me a present ? "

" It would be like him if he did," I said. " I fancy he will."

" I can't go and kick him," said my uncle.

" Declined with thanks," I suggested, " owing to pressure of other matter."

" You are getting shoppy, George," said my uncle, in as near an approach to a querulous tone as I have heard from him.

" You are getting married," I replied, with the complacency of one whose troubles are over. " But it's a horrible nuisance, anyhow. Still, the world grows wiser, and the burden is not quite so bad as it used to be. A hundred years hence——"

" I'd be willing enough to wait," said my uncle ; " but I'm not the only party in this affair."

He was willing enough to wait, perhaps, but time was inexorable. Save for one hurried interview, I did not see him again for a week, and then it was before the altar.   His garrulity had fallen from him like a garment.   He was preoccupied and a trifle bashful.   He fumbled with the ring. I felt almost as though he was my younger brother.

I stood by him to the end, and at last came the hour of parting.   I grasped his hand in silence : silently he mastered a becoming emotion.   And in silence he went from me unto the New Life.

THE gentleman with the Jovian coiffure began to speak as the train moved. "'Tis the utmost degradation of art," he said. He had apparently fallen into conversation with his companion upon the platform.

"I don't see it," said this companion, a prosperous-looking gentleman with a gold watch-chain. "This art for art's sake—I don't believe in it, I tell you. Art should have an aim. If it don't do you good, if it ain't moral, I'd as soon not have it. What good is it? I believe in Ruskin. I tell you——"

"*Bah!*" said the gentleman in the corner, with almost explosive violence. He fired it like a big gun across the path of the incipient argument, and slew the prosperous-looking gentleman at once. He met our eyes, as we turned to him,

100

with a complacent smile on his large white, clean-shaven face. He was a corpulent person, dressed in black, and with something of the quality of a second-hand bishop in his appearance. The demolished owner of the watch-chain made some beginnings of a posthumous speech.

" *Bah !* " said the gentleman in the corner, with even more force than before, and so finished him.

" These people will never understand," he said, after a momentary pause, addressing the gentleman with the Jovian coiffure, and indicating the remains of the prosperous gentleman by a wave of a large white hand. " Why do you argue ? Art is ever for the few."

" I did not argue," said the gentleman with the hair. " I was interrupted."

The owner of the watch-chain, who had been sitting struggling with his breath, now began to sob out his indignation. " What do you *mean*, sir ? Saying *Bah !* sir, when I am talking———"

The gentleman with the large face held

up a soothing hand. " Peace, peace,"
he said. " I did not interrupt you. I
annihilated you. Why did you presume
to talk to artists about art? Go away,
or I shall have to say Bah! again. Go
and have a fit. Leave us—two rare
souls who may not meet again—to our
talking."

" Did you ever see such abominable
rudeness, sir?" said the gentleman with
the watch-chain, appealing to me. There
were tears in his eyes. At the same
time the young man with the aureole
made some remark to the corpulent
gentleman that I failed to catch.

" These artists," said I, " are unac-
countable, irresponsible. You must———"

"Take it from whence it comes," said
the insulted one, very loudly, and bitterly
glaring at his opponent. But the two
artists were conversing serenely. I felt
the undignified quality of our conversation. " Have you seen *Punch*?" said I,
thrusting it into his hand.

He looked at the paper for a moment

in a puzzled way; then understood, thanked me, and began to read with a thunderous scowl, every now and then shooting murderous glances at his antagonist in the opposite corner, or coughing in an aggressive manner.

"You do your best," the gentleman with the long hair was saying; "and they say, 'What is it for?' 'It is for itself,' you say. Like the stars."

"But these people," said the stout gentleman, "think the stars were made to set their clocks by. They lack the magnanimity to drop the personal reference. A friend, a *confrère*, saw a party of these horrible Extension people at Rome before that exquisite Venus of Titian. 'And now, Mr Something-or-other,' said one of the young ladies, addressing the pedagogue in command, 'what is *this* to teach us?'"

"I have had the same experience," said the young gentleman with the hair. "A man sent to me only a week ago to ask what my sonnet 'The Scarlet Thread' *meant*?"

The stout person shook his head as though such things passed all belief.

" Gur-r-r-r," said the gentleman with *Punch*, and scraped with his foot on the floor of the carriage.

" I gave him answer," said the poet, " 'Twas a sonnet, not a symbol."

" Precisely," said the stout gentleman. .

" 'Tis the fate of all art to be misunderstood. I am always grossly misunderstood—by every one. They call me fantastic, whereas I am but inevitably new ; indecent, because I am unfettered by mere trivial personal restrictions ; unwholesome."

" It is what they say to me. They are always trying to pull me to earth. ' Is it wholesome ? ' they say ; ' nutritious ? ' I say to them, ' I do not know. I am an artist. I do not care. It is beautiful.' "

" You rhyme ? " said the poet.

" No. My work is—more plastic. I cook."

For a moment, perhaps, the poet was disconcerted. " A noble art," he said, recovering.

"The noblest," said the cook. "But sorely misunderstood ; degraded to utilitarian ends ; tested by impossible standards. I have been seriously asked to render oily food palatable to a delicate patient. Seriously ! "

"He said, ' Bah !' Bah ! to *me !* " mumbled the defunct gentleman with *Punch,* apparently addressing the cartoon. " A cook ! Good *Lord !* "

" I resigned. ' Cookery,' I said, ' is an art. I am not a fattener of human cattle. Think : Is it Art to write a book with an object, to paint a picture for strategy ? ' ' Are we,' I said, ' in the sixties or the nineties ? Here, in your kitchen, I am inspired with beautiful dinners, and I produce them. It is your place to gather together, from this place one, and from that, one, the few precious souls who can appreciate that rare and wonderful thing, a dinner, graceful, harmonious, exquisite, perfect.' And he argued I must study his guests ! "

"No artist is of any worth," said the

poet, "who primarily studies what the public needs."

"As I told him. But the next man was worse—hygienic. While with this creature I read Poe for the first time, and I was singularly fascinated by some of his grotesques. I tried—it was an altogether new development, I believe, in culinary art—the Bizarre. I made some curious arrangements in pork and strawberries, with a sauce containing beer. Quite by accident I mentioned my design to him on the evening of the festival. All the Philistine was aroused in him. ' It will ruin my digestion.' ' My friend,' I said, ' I am not your doctor ; I have nothing to do with your digestion. Only here is a beautiful Japanese thing, a quaint, queer, almost eerie dinner, that is in my humble opinion worth many digestions. You may take it or leave it, but 'tis the last dinner I cook for you.' . . . I knew I was wasted upon him.

"Then I produced some Nocturnes in imitation of Mr Whistler, with mushrooms, truffles, grilled meat, pickled walnuts, black pudding, French plums, porter— a dinner in soft velvety black, eaten in a starlight of small scattered candles. That, too, led to a resignation : Art will ever demand its martyrs."

The poet made sympathetic noises.

" Always. The awful many will never understand. Their conception of my skill is altogether on a level with their conceptions of music, of literature, of painting. For wall decorations they love autotypes ; for literature, harmless volumes of twaddle that leave no vivid impressions on the mind ; for dinners, harmless dishes that are forgotten as they are eaten. *My* dinners stick in the memory. I cannot study these people —my genius is all too imperative. If I needed a flavour of almonds and had nothing else to hand, I would use prussic acid. Do right, I say, as your art instinct commands, and take no heed of the consequences. Our function is to make the beautiful gastronomic thing, not to pander to gluttony, not to be the Jesuits of

hygiene.   My friend, you should see some
of my compositions.   At home I have
books and books in manuscript, Symphonies,
Picnics, Fantasies, *Etudes* . . ."

The train was now entering Clapham
Junction.   The gentleman with the gold
watch-chain returned my *Punch.*   " A
cook," he said in a whisper ; "just a
common cook ! " He lifted his eyebrows
and shook his head at me, and proceeded
to extricate himself and his umbrella
from the carriage.   " Out of a situation
too ! " he said—a little louder—as I prepared to follow him.

" Mere dripping ! " said the artist in
cookery, with a regal wave of the hand.

Had I felt sure I was included, I should
of course have resented the phrase.

THE MAN WITH A NOSE

"I never see thy face but I think upon hell-fire, and Dives that lived in purple, for there he is in his robes, burning, burning."

"MY nose has been the curse of my life."

The other man started.

They had not spoken before. They were sitting, one at either end, on that seat on the stony summit of Primrose Hill which looks towards Regent's Park. It was night. The paths on the slope below were dotted out by yellow lamps; the Albert-road was a line of faintly luminous pale green—the tint of gaslight seen among trees; beyond, the park lay black and mysterious, and still further, a yellow mist beneath and a coppery hue in the sky above marked the blaze of the Marylebone thoroughfares. The nearer houses in the

Albert-terrace loomed large and black, their blackness pierced irregularly by luminous windows. Above, starlight.

Both men had been silent, lost apparently in their own thoughts, mere dim black figures to each other, until one had seen fit to become a voice also, with this confidence.

"Yes," he said, after an interval, "my nose has always stood in my way, always."

The second man had scarcely seemed to notice the first remark, but now he peered through the night at his interlocutor. It was a little man he saw, with face turned towards him.

"I see nothing wrong with your nose."

"If it were luminous you might," said the first speaker. "However, I will illuminate it."

He fumbled with something in his pocket, then held this object in his hand. There was a scratch, a streak of greenish phosphorescent light, and then all the world beyond became black, as a fusee vesta flared.

There was silence for the space of a minute.   An impressive pause.

" Well ? " said the man with the nose, putting his heel on the light.

" I have seen worse," said the second man.

" I doubt it," said the man with the nose ; " and even so, it is poor comfort. Did you notice the shape ? the size ? the colour ?   Like Snowdon, it has a steep side and a gentle slope.   The size is preposterous : my face is like a hen-house built behind a portico.   And the tints ! "

" It is not all red," said the second man, " anyhow."

" No, there is purple, and blue, ' *lapis lazuli*, blue as a vein over the Madonna's breast,' and in one place a greyish mole. Bah ! the thing is not a nose at all, but a bit of primordial chaos clapped on to my face.   But, being where the nose should be, it gets the credit of its position from unthinking people.   There is a gap in the order of the universe in front of my face, a lump of unwrought material left over.   In that my true nose is hidden, as a statue is hidden in a lump of marble, until the appointed time for the revelation shall come. At the resurrection——But one must not anticipate. Well, well. I do not often talk about my nose, my friend, but you sat with a sympathetic pose, it seemed to me, and to-night my heart is full of it. This cursed nose ! But do I weary you, thrusting my nose into your meditations ? "

" If," said the second man, his voice a little unsteady, as though he was moved, " if it eases your mind to talk of your nose, pray talk."

" This nose, I say then, makes me think of the false noses of Carnival times. Your dullest man has but to stick one on, and lo ! mirth, wit, and jollity. They are enough to make anything funny. I doubt if even an Anglican bishop could wear one with impunity. Put an angel in one. How would you like one popped on to *you* now ? Think of going love-making, or addressing a public meeting, or dying gloriously, in a nose like mine ! Angelina laughs in your face, the public laughs, the executioner at your martyrdom can hardly light the faggots for laughing. By heaven ! it is no joke. Often and often I have rebelled, and said, ' I will not have this nose ! ' "

" But what can one do ? "

" It is destiny. The bitter tragedy of it is that it is so comic. Only, God knows, how glad I shall be when the Carnival is over, and I may take the thing off and put it aside. The worst has been this business of love. My mind is not unrefined, my body is healthy. I know what tenderness is. But what woman could overlook a nose like mine ? How could she shut out her visions of it, and look her love into my eyes, glaring at her over its immensity ? I should have to make love through an Inquisitor's hood, with its holes cut for the eyes—and even then the shape would show. I have read, I have been told, I can imagine what a lover's face is like— a sweet woman's face radiant with love.

But this Millbank penitentiary of flesh chills their dear hearts."

He broke off suddenly, with loud ferocious curses. A young man who had been sitting very close to a young woman on an adjacent seat, started up and said " Ssh !".

He whom the man with the nose had addressed now spoke. " I have certainly never thought before of a red nose as a sorrowful thing, but as you put it. . . ."

" I thought you would understand. I have had this nose all my life. The outline was done, even though the colour was wanting, in my school days. They called me ' Nosey,' ' Ovid,' ' Cicero,' ' Rhino,' and the ' Excrescence.' It has ripened with the slow years, as fate deepens in the progress of a tragedy. Love, the business of life, is a sealed book to me. To be alone ! I would thank heaven. . . . But no ! a blind woman could feel the shape of it."

" Besides love," interrupted the young man thoughtfully, " there are other things worth living for—duty. An unattractive nose would not interfere with that. Some people think it is rather more important than love. I admit your loss, of course."

"That only carries out the evidence of your voice, and tells me you are young. My dear young fellow, duty is a very fine thing indeed, but believe me, it is too colourless as a motive. There is no delight in duty. You will know that at my age. And besides, I have an infinite capacity for love and sympathy, an infinite bitterness in this solitude of my soul. I infer that you would moralise on my discontent, but I know I have seen a little of men and things from behind this ambuscade— only a truly artistic man would fall into the sympathetic attitude that attracted me. My life has had even too much of observation in it, and to the systematic anthropologist, nothing tells a man's character more than his pose after dark, when nobody seems watching. As you sit, the black outline of you is clear against the sky. Ah! *now* you are sitting stiffer. But you

are no Calvinist. My friend, the best of
life is its delights, and the best of delights
is loving and being loved. And for that—
this nose ! Well, there are plenty of second-
best things. After dark I can forget the
monster a little. Spring is delightful, air
on the Downs is delightful; it is fine to
see the stars circling in the sky, while
lying among the heather. Even this
London sky is soothing at night, though
the edge is all inflamed. The shadow of
my nose is darkest by day. But to-night
I am bitter, because of to-morrow."

"Why, to-morrow ?" said the younger
man.

"I have to meet some new people to-
morrow," said the man with the nose.
"There is an odd look, a mingling of
amusement and pity, I am only too familiar
with. My cousin, who is a gifted hostess,
promises people my nose as a treat."

"Yes, that must be bad for you," said
the young man.

And then the silence healed again, and
presently the man with the nose got up

and passed into the dimness upon the slope of the hill. The young man watched him vanish, wondering vainly how it would be possible to console a soul under such a burthen.

TURNBULL AND SPEARS, PRINTERS, EDINBURGH